THE CHOCOLATE . . . POTATO CHIP!

He took a small piece of potato chip, tilted back his head until he was looking straight up at the ceiling, and dropped the morsel straight down into his throat. He felt it go down, a sharp fragment of sweet chocolate. He tried the milk, the ice water, the fruit. Every solid and liquid that he sampled was transformed as soon as it entered his mouth.

PATRICK
SKENE
CATLING

The Chocolate Touch

Illustrated Edition
Pictures by Margot Apple

A BANTAM SKYLARK BOOK®
TORONTO · NEW YORK · LONDON · SYDNEY

*This low-priced Bantam Book
has been completely reset in a type face
designed for easy reading, and was printed
from new plates. It contains the complete
text of the original hard-cover edition.*
NOT ONE WORD HAS BEEN OMITTED.

RL 3, IL 3+

THE CHOCOLATE TOUCH
*A Bantam Book / published by arrangement with
William Morrow & Co., Inc.*

PRINTING HISTORY
*William Morrow edition published September 1952
Illustrated edition published February 1979

Bantam Skylark edition / April 1981*

*Bantam Books are published by Bantam Books, Inc. Its trade-
mark, consisting of the words "Bantam Books" and the por-
trayal of a bantam, is Registered in U.S. Patent and Trademark
Office and in other countries. Marca Registrada. Bantam
Books, Inc., 666 Fifth Avenue, New York, New York 10103.*

PRINTED IN THE UNITED STATES OF AMERICA

0 9 8

For Sheila, Ellen, Charlotte,
and Desmond.

The Chocolate Touch

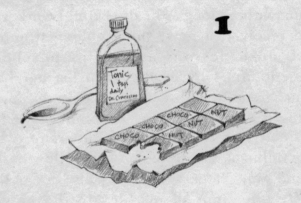

1

Most of the time John Midas was a very nice boy. Every now and then, of course, he broke a rule, such as the rule against pretending to be a tiger when his sister, Mary, was supposed to be getting to sleep. Generally speaking, however, he behaved very well.

He should have behaved better.

He lived in a comfortable house surrounded by a green lawn and wide-spreading shade trees that were suitable for climbing. His mother was gentle as well as practical. His father, when he didn't have to hurry to town, spent hours telling John interesting things about baseball, beetles, birds' nests, boats, brigands, and butterflies.

John went to school and liked it. His teacher, Miss Plimsole, was fairly easy to get along with, as long as he did careful work. He had received a new, shiny golden trumpet and music lessons as a going-to-school present. Mrs. Quaver, the music teacher, had soon agreed to let him play small parts, a few notes at a time, with the school orchestra.

Finally, there was Susan Buttercup, who was in his class. Susan had soft yellow curls, round pink cheeks, blue eyes, and one of the best collections of marbles in the neighborhood.

John should have been completely well-behaved. But he wasn't.

He had one bad fault: he was a pig about candy. Boiled candy, cotton candy, licorice all-sorts, old-fashioned toffee, candied or-

ange and lemon slices, Cracker Jack, jelly beans, fudge, black-currant lozenges for ticklish throats, nougat, *marrons glacés,* acid drops, peppermint sticks, lollipops, marshmallows, and, above all, chocolates—he devoured them all.

While other boys and girls spent their money on model airplanes, magazines, skipping ropes, and pet lizards, John studied the candy counters. All his money went on candy, and all his candy went to himself. He never shared it. John Midas was candy mad.

At lunch one Saturday Mrs. Midas noticed a couple of little red spots on the end of John's nose. "Look," she said to Mr. Midas. "John has spots."

Mr. Midas leaned forward to look at them. He gravely shook his head and clicked his tongue. John tried to look too. But it is very difficult to see the end of your own nose without a mirror unless you happen to be an elephant with a long nose that you can bend double. When John tried to look at the end of his nose, first with one eye and then with the other, and then with both together, all that he could see was a pink blur. Besides, trying to look at something so close made his eyes ache.

"I can't see any spots, Mother," John said.

"Well, I can," Mr. Midas said. "Just because you don't see a thing doesn't always mean it isn't there. Try feeling the end of your nose with your finger."

John rubbed his finger over the tip of his nose. It felt a bit rough.

"It may be measles," Mrs. Midas said anxiously. She placed her hand on John's forehead to feel whether he was warmer than usual. "But I don't think he has a temperature," she decided.

"I suspect John has been eating too much candy again," Mr. Midas said. "Have you been eating candy this morning, John?"

"Some," John admitted.

"What?" Mr. Midas asked.

"Well," John replied. "Well . . . I had a few Cream Delights. Susan gave them to me."

"Anything else?" Mr. Midas asked.

"A little Toffee Crunch," John said.

"And what else?" Mr. Midas asked, beginning to look cross.

John's ears grew red. He knew he wasn't

supposed to eat candy before meals. "Oh, only, er, oh . . . hardly anything else," he said.

"John!" Mr. Midas said, and his son recognized the tone. It meant that John had to tell everything.

It turned out that John had been around to see most of his friends and had managed to get candy from nearly all of them. The list he recited was a long one.

"No wonder you have spots," Mr. Midas commented at last. "I think we'd better take John to see Dr. Cranium," he said to Mrs. Midas.

Dr. Cranium was a tall, thin man with a bald head and a gray mustache. He looked through his glasses at John and said, "Hmm."

"He eats a lot of candy," Mr. Midas said.

"He hasn't been eating his meals properly," Mrs. Midas said.

"That's just what I thought," Dr. Cranium said. "I can tell by looking at him that he eats much too much candy." The doctor shone a little electric light into John's right ear. Then he shone it into John's left ear. Then he shone it in John's nose. He told John to open wide and say *ah*. Then he shone the light into

John's mouth. "Much too much candy! Gracious me—he seems to be full of candy!"

He told John to sit down and relax. Then he picked up a small rubber-headed hammer and gave John a light tap on the right knee, just below the joint. John's foot gave a weak kick. John giggled.

"It's nothing to laugh about," Mr. Midas said.

"No, John," the doctor reproved him. "A healthy little boy who didn't eat too much candy would kick harder than that."

"I'm sorry," John said politely. "But I can kick harder if you want me to." He gave a sudden high kick, which knocked the hammer out of Dr. Cranium's hand. It landed on its rubber head and bounced across the room.

"John!" exclaimed Mrs. Midas. "I'm so sorry, Dr. Cranium. John, tell the doctor you're sorry for kicking his hammer."

"I'm sorry I kicked your hammer," John said.

"I would recommend less candy," Dr. Cranium told Mr. and Mrs. Midas. "An upset stomach can lead to all sorts of complications."

On the way home Mrs. Midas tried to explain to John what she thought the doctor meant by complications. "You see," she said, "if you put too much of one kind of food in your stomach and not enough of other kinds, it is bad for your whole body, because different parts of your body need different kinds of food. Do you understand?"

"I think so," John said.

"You've been eating so much sweet stuff," Mr. Midas added, "that there isn't room for eggs and meat and milk and bread and spinach and apples and fish and bananas and all the other things you're supposed to have to make you grow big and strong."

"I like bananas," John said. "Especially in thin slices covered with chocolate. They're called Banana Surprises."

Mr. Midas looked at Mrs. Midas, and Mrs. Midas looked at Mr. Midas. They both shrugged their shoulders. Sometimes it was hard to make John understand things.

At home, while Mrs. Midas was busy in the kitchen, Mr. Midas continued to reason with John. "You mean you'd rather eat candy than anything else, and chocolate rather than any other kind of candy?" Mr. Midas asked.

"Yes!" John assured him. "Oh, yes!"

"Don't you think there's such a thing as enough?" Mr. Midas persisted. "Don't you think that things are best in their places? I mean, don't you think there's a time for spaghetti and a time for roast beef and even a time for pickled herring and garlic toast, as well as a time for chocolate? Or would you rather have chocolate all the time?"

"Chocolate all the time," John replied emphatically. "Chocolate's best, that's all. Other things are just food. But chocolate's chocolate. Chocolate—"

"I think I understand," Mr. Midas broke in sharply. "Very well." He took a deep breath and went on. "John," he said, "if you can't understand what sort of diet is really best for you, can't you at least get it into your head that you make your mother very unhappy when you eat so much candy that you can't eat anything else?"

The conversation always seemed to get around to the effect of John's candy eating on John's mother. John couldn't see how it could possibly do her any harm if he ate candy.

He sat silent for a moment. Then he said, "May I go out and play, please, Daddy?"

2

It was Sunday afternoon. The sun was sinking low in the sky, but the air was still quite warm. John was wandering along in the direction of Susan's house, absentmindedly looking down at the sidewalk, when his eye was suddenly caught by a dully gleaming, silvery gray coin lying right in his path.

The coin was the size of a quarter. But even as he leaned forward eagerly to pick it up, John noticed there was something strange about it. It did not have a picture of George Washington or a picture of an eagle. On one side there was a picture of a fat boy; on the other side were the letters *J.M.*—which was funny, John thought, because those letters happened to be his initials.

Grasping the coin firmly, he ran on toward Susan's house. She liked to collect things. He thought she might be interested to know that he had the beginning of a coin collection.

Although he was in the habit of going over to Susan's by the same route once or twice almost every day, this afternoon John found himself turning left where he usually turned right.

I always go the same way, he thought. This time, for a change, I'm going a new way.

He didn't stop to consider that you cannot go east by going west, unless you go all the way around the world.

Only two blocks along the unfamiliar

street, John came to a small corner store. It was a neat red-brick building with two big show windows. They were full of all sorts of candy. Susan was immediately, absolutely forgotten. John pressed his nose against one of the windows. He was imagining the taste of the chocolate-covered almonds and chocolate fudge on the other side of the glass when he noticed a man in a white apron standing behind the counter and beckoning to him. John was surprised. He hadn't expected the store to be open on Sunday.

"Don't just stand there in the doorway, John," the man called heartily. "Come on in and get some fresh, sweet, creamy chocolate. There's a special sale today."

How did the man know his name? John wondered. He couldn't remember ever having seen the store before.

The storekeeper saw John hesitate. "The chocolate I use in my kitchen comes direct from the heart of Africa," he said. "I use none but the finest ingredients. And my recipes—! Well, I bet you've never had chocolates like mine before. Come on in."

"Thank you," John replied, walking to the

counter. "But you see the trouble is . . . well
. . ."

"No money?" the storekeeper asked. "No money whatsoever? What've you got there in your right hand?"

John had forgotten the old coin in his hand. "Oh," he said, "this is part of my coin collection. I mean," he added more honestly, "I'm going to save this coin and then get some more to make a collection."

"Let me have a look at it," the storekeeper said. He looked briefly at the coin. "Aha!" he exclaimed.

"Is it any good?" John asked, his hopes suddenly rising.

"Very good," said the storekeeper. "In fact, it's the only kind of money I accept. But I don't suppose that you'd want to spend it on a box—"

"A whole box?"

"I imagine you'd rather keep this for your coin collection than spend it on chocolate, wouldn't you?"

"Oh, no!" John said. "Chocolate any day!"

"Go ahead then. Help yourself," the storekeeper said, pointing to a heavily laden show table piled high with large cellophane-wrapped candy boxes, all exactly alike.

"You mean I can have one of *these?*" John asked, his eyes round with surprise. The candy boxes were as big as the ones his father always brought home at Christmastime.

"Just help yourself," the storekeeper assured him. "That is, unless you think it might be better to ask your mother first."

"She wouldn't mind," John said hastily, and blushed.

The storekeeper winked knowingly. "I'm sure she won't," he agreed. "Not in the long run, anyway."

John tucked one of the large boxes under his arm, declined the storekeeper's offer to wrap it as a gift, thanked him, and hurried out of the store before there could be any question of anyone's changing his mind.

The storekeeper smiled as he watched his customer hurrying away down the street.

John decided that it might be sensible to enter his house quietly by way of the kitchen. With the large candy box hidden behind him, he let himself in by the back door and crept up the kitchen stairway on tiptoe toward his own room on the top floor. Just as he was about to round the corner on the second floor to continue his way upstairs, he had to stop for a moment while his father walked by, coming along the hall from the bedroom telephone.

"That was Mrs. Buttercup on the phone," Mr. Midas called to Mrs. Midas, as he walked down the front stairs. "She said she was sorry John hasn't been able to get over to play with Susan this afternoon. But it was a good thing in a way, she thought, because Susan's already so excited about her birthday party tomorrow. I wonder where John can have got to."

As soon as the second floor was quiet again and John knew there was no danger that his candy box would be seen, he hurried silently up to his bedroom, pushed open the door, and slid the box under the bed. Then he walked heavily down to the living room.

"Well, there you are," said Mrs. Midas. "We couldn't imagine where you had been. What have you been doing?"

"Oh, just sort of playing around," John said.

* * *

John usually took a long time to put his things away and undress and bathe and get ready for bed, for he thought sleeping was a waste of time. But this evening he started yawning long before his usual bedtime.

"Ho, hum. Ho-o-o, hum-m-m. Sleepy," John announced.

"All right," said Mrs. Midas. "You'd better be getting to bed. Time for your tonic."

John's tonic came in a bottle. It had been prescribed by Dr. Cranium. John had to drink a big spoonful every night to make up for all the vegetables and fruit that he left on his plate at lunch and dinner. The tonic tasted like soap, mud, glue, ink, and paint. It tasted horrible.

Much to Mrs. Midas' surprise, John ran ahead of her to the dining-room cupboard where the tonic and the tonic spoon were kept. By the time she got there he had already filled the spoon. Then, without any coaxing, he emptied it into his mouth.

"Ugh!" John spluttered. "Oof! Baw!"

"That's a very good boy," Mrs. Midas said. "Now why can't you be sensible and eat up your nice dinner that way? If you'd only stop eating so much candy, you'd be able to eat your meals properly and you wouldn't need to take the tonic."

Soon John was scrubbed and in his pajamas and in bed, ready to be tucked in for the night. Mrs. Midas sat on the bed and stroked his forehead for a moment. Then she leaned forward and kissed his cheek. John, pretending that he was very sleepy, shut his eyes and began breathing deeply.

When Mrs. Midas rejoined Mr. Midas in the living room, she said, "I've never known John to be so good about going to bed before. He went to sleep in no time."

A few seconds after the bedroom door had closed behind his mother, John leaped to the floor, got down on his hands and knees, and felt under the bed for the candy box. He soon had it on the pillow and set to work unfastening it. First he took off the thin outer sheet of cellophane. Then he lifted off the lid. Then he removed a sheet of cardboard. Then he pulled off a square of heavy tinfoil. Then he took out a layer of shredded paper.

As the wrappings piled up around him, John became rather anxious. At last he came to a small central ball of cotton batting, and there, right in the middle, was a little golden ball. He picked at the ball with his fingernail and peeled away the gold paper, revealing a tiny piece of plain chocolate. It was the only piece of chocolate in the whole box.

Deeply disappointed, John nevertheless put it into his mouth. He had never tasted a chocolate quite like it. It was the most chocolaty chocolate he had ever encountered.

3

The birds were chirping in the tree outside John's window, and the sky beyond was deep blue. The bedroom door opened a few inches. "Hey, sleepy!" Mrs. Midas called. "Everyone else is up!"

John put on his bathrobe and slippers and

ambled to the bathroom. His sister, Mary, was still brushing her teeth, and he had to wait until she finished.

"Come on, Mary," he said a little crossly. "Don't take all morning."

"Here you are," Mary said, handing him the toothpaste tube.

While Mary soaped her face, John squeezed a little of the toothpaste onto his brush. The paste was pink. John made a face at his toothbrush. It didn't seem fair that he should have to brush his teeth with stuff that tasted just like his tonic. "A stinky taste," he called it.

John opened his mouth and pushed in the end of the toothbrush. As soon as it touched his front teeth, he noticed a delicious sweetness in his mouth, a taste of the best kind of chocolate. He pushed the brush to and fro, and the taste seemed to grow stronger. He removed the brush. The bristles were brown.

"What kind of toothpaste is this?" John asked.

Mary was drying her face. "The same kind," she answered. "It says on the tube."

"Blanco-Dent," John read. It was the same kind they had always had.

"Why's it chocolate-flavored this time?" he asked. "Boy, it's good!"

"Silly!" Mary said. " 'Course it isn't chocolate!" She hung up her towel and swished out of the bathroom.

John squeezed some more toothpaste onto his brush and continued to brush his teeth. Chocolate again! It was marvelous—rich, sweet, smooth chocolate, chocolaty chocolate, like the single piece of chocolate from the box the night before.

There seemed to be no further need for the toothbrush, so John rinsed it and hung it up. He squeezed out another bit of toothpaste, onto a fingertip this time. He put his finger in his mouth and ate the toothpaste off. When he took his finger out again, it was stained chocolate brown. John wasted no more time. He put the end of the toothpaste tube into his mouth and emptied the paste onto his tongue. It squeezed out like thick, creamy chocolate.

Mary looked into the bathroom. "Hey, what are you doing?" she demanded.

"Yummy!" was all John said.

John and Mary were a little late getting to the dining room, and Mr. Midas was already on the way to his train when they sat down at the breakfast table.

"John ate up all the toothpaste," Mary told their mother.

"Ooh, you sneak!" John whispered.

"Well, you did," Mary reminded him. "And that's a waste. Isn't it a waste, Mother, to eat up all the toothpaste in one day?"

Mrs. Midas was serving their orange juice. "Mary really!" she cried. "I'm sure John was only joking. He must have been pretending to eat the toothpaste."

"No, he wasn't," Mary insisted. "I was watching, and I saw him squeeze it right into his mouth. He said it was chocolate."

"Oh, dear," protested Mrs. Midas. "Chocolate again! Now I know it was just a joke. He just wished it were chocolate, Mary. Come now, drink up your orange juice, both of you. Your bacon and eggs will be ready in a minute."

As Mrs. Midas left the room, John took up his glass of orange juice and put it to his lips. As soon as he tilted it and the liquid began to flow into his mouth, a happy look came into his eyes. "Boy, that's good," he said at last, lowering the empty glass. "Chocolate juice."

Mary looked at John. Then she looked at her glass of orange juice. It was a bright orange color. She tasted it. It tasted like orange to her. "It is *not* chocolate juice," she said. "It's orange juice. Orange juice is good for you."

"Yes, John," Mrs. Midas said, hearing the last few words as she carried in the tray of bacon and eggs. "You must drink your—" She caught sight of John's empty glass. "John," she said, "you good boy! That's the first time in ages you've finished your orange juice without having to be told to."

"It tasted of chocolate," John explained.

"All right," Mrs. Midas said. "Very funny. But don't tease Mary too much. Remember—Mary's younger than you are."

John silently picked up his fork and sliced the yoke of his fried egg. The yellow broke over the white and he shivered as he watched it, as he always did. "I can't eat this," he told his mother.

"Of course you can," Mrs. Midas said. "You drank your orange juice. Try to eat your bacon and egg."

John scraped up a small piece of egg and put it into his mouth. It immediately became chocolate—chocolate white and chocolate yolk. Both lovely, lovely chocolate. "Mmm!" John mumbled. "Chocolate egg!" In almost no time he had finished every scrap of egg on his plate. Then he tried the bacon. The bacon turned to chocolate, too.

John had never before enjoyed his breakfast so much. After the orange juice that had turned to chocolate juice in his mouth and the fried bacon and egg that had turned to fried chocolate, he ate two slices of chocolate toast with chocolate butter and chocolate marmalade, washed down with a glass of chocolate milk.

"I'm very pleased with you this morning," Mrs. Midas said, as she helped John on with his coat. "If you promise to eat your lunch at school as well as you ate your breakfast, I'll give you a dime to buy some chocolates with."

"Oh, that's all right," John said. "I don't think I'll need it."

Mrs. Midas looked puzzled as she waved good-bye.

4

John had the bad habit of chewing things when he was thinking hard. This morning he had several things to think about. What had made the toothpaste taste like chocolate? What had made the orange juice taste like chocolate? What had made the bacon and egg taste like chocolate? What had made the toast and butter and marmalade taste like chocolate?

Each one of these things had felt the way it had always felt before. The toothpaste had been soft and pasty. The bacon had been hot, crisp, and oily. The toast had been crunchy and the marmalade sticky and lumpy. But everything had tasted like the chocolate he had eaten in bed last night.

John put a gloved thumb in his mouth and thoughtfully chewed. His mother had frequently pointed out to him that chewing his gloves made little holes that let in the cold air. But he chewed them just the same when he was thinking hard. This time he noticed something very queer about the thumb of his glove. Instead of tasting leathery, it tasted like chocolate. John pulled his thumb out of his mouth. The part of the glove that had been in his mouth was now brown, instead of black like the rest.

He bit the end of the leather thumb again. It came right off in his mouth, leaving his own thumb bare. John chewed, and it was like chewing leather made of chocolate, leather that melted like chocolate. . . . In a second or two he swallowed it.

The gloves were not new. John had had them quite a while. He couldn't understand why he had never thought of eating them before. He tried to tear off one of the fingers, but the leather was too strong for him. He put it into his mouth, and it immediately turned into chocolate. Then he was able to break it off easily. He popped it into his mouth and chewed it up and swallowed it. It was delicious.

Walking along devouring his glove, John did not notice one of his schoolfellows, Spider Wilson, until he heard his voice. "John's gone crazy! John's gone crazy!" Spider yelled. Then he turned on John. "Don't they feed you where you live?" He sneered. Spider was in the grade just above John's and was one of the meanest and slyest boys in the whole school.

John gulped down a large piece of the second glove's palm and looked pleased.

"What's the matter?" Spider demanded. "Do your people make you eat leather?"

"This is special leather," John replied. He

licked his lips and sighed contentedly. "It turns into chocolate as soon as you put it into your mouth. Look." John bit off the glove's little finger and took it out of his mouth. "Now it's chocolate." He put it back into his mouth and gulped it down.

"Give me a piece," Spider said.

"Why should I?" John wanted to know. "They're my gloves."

"Hand over a piece," Spider said.

"Do I eat your gloves?" John asked reasonably, his mouth full of chocolate. "Why should you eat mine?"

"Those aren't real gloves," Spider said. "Whenever one person has candy, he has to share it with the others. That's the club rule."

"What club?" John asked.

"Never mind what club," Spider said. "But you'd better let me have some of that chocolate."

Without waiting longer, Spider snatched what was left of the second glove. John was too surprised to resist, and he didn't want to, anyhow. He had a feeling that he'd had enough chocolate for a while. He was getting a bit thirsty.

Spider ran only a little way ahead. When he

saw that John wasn't going to fight to get the glove back, he started to eat his prize. He stuffed the leather into his mouth and took a big bite. Spider stopped short in his tracks. He frowned and bit deep into the leather again. Disgusting! It tasted worse than just leather. It tasted like leather with which a boy had made mud pies and snowballs and patted old dogs.

John thought perhaps he might be getting late for school, so he started running. He left Spider Wilson spitting the soggy remains of the glove into the gutter.

Still giggling to himself about the defeat of the enemy, John walked between the great stone pillars at the entrance to the school grounds. He had gone no more than halfway to the main building when he heard Susan Buttercup calling him. She was standing near the jungle gym with some of her friends.

"I've got something to show you, John," she shouted.

As she came running to meet him, he could see that she was waving something in her hand that flashed as it caught the rays of the sun. It was a silver dollar. "It's a birthday present!" she explained, showing him the dollar. "Isn't it beautiful?"

The sight of such wealth made John forget the triumphs of his own day. "It's a good present," he said. "Are you sure it's made of silver, though? I once got a whole bag of gold coins in a Christmas stocking, only they were chocolate coins covered with gold paper."

"Of course it's real, silly," Susan said. "My daddy said so. You can feel it if you don't believe me." She handed him the coin.

John looked at the coin suspiciously.

"All right," Susan said. "Bite it, if you think it isn't real. Go on, bite it!"

John felt rather silly. "I can see it's real now," he said. "I don't have to bite it."

"But I want you to," Susan insisted. "You weren't sure. Well, *make* sure. That's what they always do on television. When a cowboy wants to make sure a dollar's real, he bites it."

John put the dollar about halfway into his mouth and reluctantly bit it. His teeth went right through the coin. The part that had passed between his lips was hard but sweet chocolate.

Susan could hardly believe her eyes. She

had given John a complete circle of silver. He sadly handed back a crescent.

John didn't know what to say. Susan couldn't speak. Tears trickled down her cheeks like rain down a windowpane. She looked at the piece of dollar in her hand. She looked up at John, whose face was red with embarrassment. "John Midas," Susan blurted out at last, "I hate you." She turned and ran away before John could think of anything at all to say.

5

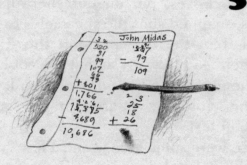

John hung up his coat, got his notebook and pencil out of his locker, and sat down at his small table just in time for the second bell, when Miss Plimsole walked silently into the classroom. As soon as she appeared in the doorway, all the chattering and scuffling stopped. The twenty boys and girls sat straight in their chairs and looked straight ahead at the clean blackboard.

"Good morning, children," Miss Plimsole said.

"Good morning, Miss Plimsole," the class answered respectfully.

Miss Plimsole sat at her high desk, blinking her eyes as she surveyed the room. Then she opened a little drawer in her desk and pulled out a spectacles case, from which she took her reading glasses. She removed her long-distance glasses, put on her short-distance glasses, snapped shut the spectacles case, replaced it in the drawer, shut the drawer, tilted her head forward so that she could look over the glasses on her nose, and said, "This morning, children, we are going to have an important test."

There were some groans and a few "ooh's" and "ah's."

Miss Plimsole lifted up one of her hands and silence was restored instantly. "No complaining, please!" she said sternly. "This test will show me how well you have been learning your arithmetic this year. It will be a short one. I am going to write just four problems on the board. I shall expect you to solve them all swiftly and accurately and to write your answers neatly. You will place your paper in front of you now. You will write your name at the top right-hand corner. And then you will place your pencil beside your paper, sit back in your chair, and wait until I give the signal to begin work." Miss Plimsole turned to the blackboard and began chalking up the test problems.

Tests always made John nervous. Besides, his lips were feeling dry, and the taste of chocolate was strong in his mouth. He raised his hand.

"Yes, John?" Miss Plimsole asked.

"Please may I go and get a drink of water, please, Miss Plimsole?" he asked in a small voice.

"Very well. Hurry back. We're going to start in a few minutes."

John gratefully slipped out of the room and walked quickly down the quiet corridor to a water fountain. His tongue felt thick with chocolate. The cold water would be refreshing.

He pressed his foot down on the fountain treadle, and a stream of clear, ice-cold water spurted up from the silver nozzle in the white enamel basin. He lowered his head until the jet of water reached his lips. The cold water splashed delightfully against the outside of his mouth. He opened his lips. As soon as the water gushed in, it turned into ice-cold chocolate water, thin and sweet.

Quickly stopping the flow, John looked with dismay at the shallow puddle that had formed and was now draining away in the basin of the fountain. He hurried to another fountain, on the second floor of the building. But there the same thing happened. The clear, ice-cold water turned to liquid chocolate in his mouth.

When John finally got back to his classroom, all the other pupils were bent over their tables, busily scratching away. Miss Plimsole looked up from her book as John tiptoed in. She looked at the clock on the wall, looked back at him, and wagged her finger reprovingly.

John began on the first of the four problems, but he was so worried about the chocolate water that he couldn't keep his mind on his work. By the time he was ready to start the fourth problem, the other boys and girls were already putting down their pencils and straightening up and smiling at each other.

"Two minutes to go," said Miss Plimsole.

Concentrating hard, John took the end of his pencil between his teeth and began to nibble it. It immediately turned to chocolate. Then he noticed an even more disturbing change. Although he had taken the pencil out of his mouth as soon as the first piece of chocolate had crumbled off, the pencil was continuing to change to chocolate. The chocolate was slowly but steadily, moving down the pencil, replacing the wood and the lead inside, changing it into a chocolate pencil before John's very eyes. The magic—for John now knew that his power must be magic—was apparently getting stronger.

By the time the whole pencil had changed from red, yellow, and black to dark brown, Miss Plimsole was announcing that only a few seconds remained in which to write down the final answer.

"Just a minute," John pleaded.

"Sh!" Miss Plimsole cautioned him, holding a finger up to her mouth.

"Sh!" chorused the slow workers, who were becoming almost as excited as John. But

John felt worst of all. He felt sure that he could finish the problem and write down the correct answer, if only he had something to write with.

"But Miss Plimsole," he begged in a loud whisper, "my pencil's turned to chocolate!"

"Hush, John!" Miss Plimsole said. "I'll speak to you after the bell."

John tried to write with his changed pencil. But the point was too soft, and he only succeeded in making a chocolate smear where he should have written 72.

6

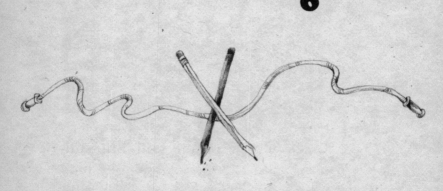

When the others had been excused to go out for midmorning play, John had to go stand by Miss Plimsole's desk.

"John," Miss Plimsole said, "you mustn't make up silly stories to excuse your failures. I must have the truth. What did you do with your pencil?"

"This is it," John said, showing Miss Plimsole the pointed stick of chocolate. "Really it is. It's changed."

"What do you mean, it's changed?" Miss Plimsole demanded.

"That's my pencil," John tried to explain, "only it isn't the same anymore. Nothing stays the same today if I put it into my mouth. The same thing happened when I chewed my gloves. They were chocolate, too."

"John," said Miss Plimsole slowly, "do . . . you . . . feel . . . all . . . right?"

"Yes, thank you," John said. "I feel all right. Except," he added, "I'm getting so thirsty. The water from the water fountain turned to chocolate and so did the water upstairs. I would like a drink of cold water."

"Yes, John," Miss Plimsole said. She suddenly looked pale. "You run out and play with the others. I'm going to have a talk with the nurse. And John," Miss Plimsole said, as he started toward the classroom door, "here's another pencil. Be a good boy and try not to lose it. I'm afraid I'll have to keep this piece of chocolate until school's out. You know we don't allow anyone to eat candy in class."

Miss Plimsole put the slightly chewed chocolate pencil in her desk drawer, and John went out to look for Susan. He found her skipping rope with two girls in his class.

John usually scorned skipping rope. He preferred hide-and-seek, tag, F.B.I. and spies, kick the can, or any other good, exciting game. Jumping up and down in one place just to avoid being hit by a rope seemed silly to him. But he was sorry for having spoiled Susan's silver dollar, and he was willing to make a sacrifice.

"Susan," he said.

Susan continued to bounce on one foot as her two friends swung the rope, over and under, over and under, over and under her. She didn't seem to notice John.

"I'll skip with you," he offered.

Susan stopped, and the rope was caught by her shins. "Let's try doubles, backward," she said, but not to John. She ignored John. "You go first, Betty. Ellen, you go second. I'll go last. The one who does it the most times gets the first slice of my birthday cake."

Susan looked at John, raised her eyebrows,

shut her eyes, and stuck out the tip of her pink tongue. Then she turned back to the girls and smiled. Ellen whispered in Betty's ear, and Betty whispered in Susan's ear. Then all three of them looked at John and at each other again and burst out laughing.

"Oh, Susan!" John protested. "I didn't mean to do it. The trouble is there's something magic about me today. Everything I put into my mouth turns to chocolate."

The girls giggled.

"You wouldn't like it," said John, who was beginning to feel sorrier for himself than he had ever felt before. "I think it's getting worse," he added reproachfully. "At first just the part in my mouth turned to chocolate. But when I nibbled the end of my pencil, the whole pencil changed."

"Pooh," Susan said. The others hooted with glee.

"Maybe I'll get sick and die," John warned. "Maybe I'll turn to chocolate myself. Then you'll be sorry."

"I don't believe one word about the chocolate," Susan said. "And if it was true, you'd be glad, because all you ever like eating is chocolate."

"If you don't believe me," John retorted, "just you give me that skipping rope and I'll prove it."

The girls looked questioningly at each other for an instant. But as they hesitated, the bell rang and it was time to go back to the classroom.

The rest of the morning passed slowly for John. He was afraid that his mother was going to be cross about the missing gloves. She might not accept the excuse that he had eaten them. He regretted his messed-up arithmetic test. He was sad about Susan's anger and disbelief. And he was getting terribly thirsty. Once during geography and once during art he was excused to get a drink of water. Both times, however, he swallowed nothing but sweet chocolate. His mouth was getting stickier and sweeter and drier by the minute.

7

"All right, boys and girls," Miss Plimsole
said. "It is almost time for lunch. Clear up
your things: paint pots securely closed,
brushes washed, paintings unpinned and laid
out to dry, drawing boards stacked against the
wall. Ah! There's the bell! Front row first,

Timothy leading, then Robin, in single file—go!"

John, alone, walked slowly in the throng hurrying along the corridors to the school cafeteria.

The school was proud of the cafeteria and the food served in it. The room was spacious and bright, with windows all the way along one side overlooking the playground and the playing fields beyond. The opposite side was wholly taken up by the shiny silver service counter.

Several boys and girls were already settled at tables by the time John took his place in the line. Enviously John noticed a boy at a nearby table suck at straws dipped in a milk bottle that was dull with frost. John could imagine the refreshing taste of cold, creamy milk. At another table a group of girls were eating fat red cherries. John could almost feel the firm fruit on his tongue and the pleasure of biting through the tart, juicy pulp. The cherries must taste good. They must be thirst quenching!

John unhappily took a tray from the pile and slid it along the rails in front of the top of the counter. He put a paper napkin, a glass and a gleaming spoon, a knife and a fork on the tray. It seemed hardly worth the while, but he felt that he might as well try the food and drink.

"Perhaps if I eat a different way, without letting anything touch my lips," he muttered, "my lunch won't all change to chocolate." He was not very hopeful.

"What?" asked the boy standing next to him.

"Nothing," John said.

"I thought I heard you say something about chocolate," the boy said. "I hope this is the day for chocolate cream pie," he added. "That'd be super."

On chocolate-cream-pie days of the past, John had been known to skip the main course, so that he might spend all his lunch money on dessert. The thought of four pieces of chocolate cream pie now suddenly made his stomach feel as though he were on a roller coaster—an uneasy, flibberty-jibberty sensation. John shuddered. "Ooky," he commented, wrinkling up his nose.

The other boy shrugged his shoulders and started to choose his meal.

John took a plate of cold chicken and ham,

potato chips, and a crisp, moist lettuce-and-tomato salad. The white of the chicken, the pink of the ham, the gold of the potatoes, the pale green of the lettuce, and the red of the tomato looked delicious. He also took a half pint of milk, a thick-crusted whole-wheat roll and a cool pat of butter, a tumbler of water with ice cubes clinking against the glass, and a dish of fresh fruit—slices of orange and grapefruit and banana and grapes.

John's tray was loaded with just the sort of meal his mother was always trying to persuade him to eat. Until today John had always thought it was pretty dull to eat "sensible things" when there were sweeter food and drink to be had. Today, however, the "sensible things" looked most appetizing, and his mouth began to water in its new sticky way.

John paid for the lunch with the money his mother had given him, went to an empty table, and sat down.

His fingers trembling slightly with eagerness, he cut a slice of lettuce. His fork went through the leaves with a promising crunch. He stuck the prongs of the fork into a mouth-sized piece of lettuce and carefully inserted it into his mouth. The lettuce didn't touch his

wide-stretched lips. John's teeth came together in crisp layers of sweet chocolate.

He took a small piece of potato chip, tilted back his head until he was looking straight up at the ceiling, and dropped the morsel straight down into his throat. He felt it go down, a sharp fragment of sweet chocolate. He tried the milk, the ice water, the fruit. Every solid and liquid that he sampled was transformed as soon as it entered his mouth.

Then he became aware of a shocking novelty that he hadn't noticed at breakfast. At the rim of each glass there was a small semicircle of opaque brown; the bowl of his spoon and the prongs of his fork had become brown. As John watched, horrified, the areas of magic chocolate slowly spread until at last the glasses and cutlery were all solid chocolate. The trouble was unquestionably growing worse.

John's scalp tightened with fear. "What am I going to do?" he asked himself miserably. "Oh, dear, oh, dear! What is going to happen to me?" Leaving his tray of chocolate food and drink and utensils, John stumbled away from the cafeteria and out to the playground.

8

English class passed without incident. Miss Plimsole distributed word lists for her pupils to take home. "The more words you know," she explained, as always, "the more exactly you can think."

There were some difficult new words, John

noticed: avarice, indigestion, acidity, unhealthiness, moderation, digestibility. As Miss Plimsole explained the meaning of each one, it seemed to John as though they all had a special bearing on his present uncomfortable condition.

At last the bell rang. "Very well, class," Miss Plimsole said. "Time for outside activities. Good afternoon."

"Good afternoon, Miss Plimsole."

Miss Plimsole gave the signal for dismissal, and the pupils in the front row filed out, followed by those in the second row, including John and Susan.

Susan played a violin in the school orchestra, and usually she and John went to the rehearsals in the auditorium together. This time Susan hurried on ahead of him. John followed very slowly.

The members of the orchestra were sitting at their music stands on the auditorium stage when John, carrying his dark-blue trumpet case, got to his chair in the brass section. Mrs. Quaver had already begun to explain a difficult passage to the girl who played the flute.

"Just after Jay sings, '. . . nestlings chirp and flee,'" she was saying, "you come in with your trill—*doodle-oodle-oodle-oodle—oo.* Do you see the place on your score? Good.

"Ah, John," Mrs. Quaver exclaimed, seeing him in his place. "I'm glad you're not absent. As I have just told the others, this afternoon we're having the first joint rehearsal of my arrangement of 'A Boy's Song,' by James Hogg.

"We've been over all the individual parts and all the sections, you will recall. Now it's time to fit the pieces together."

John nervously opened his trumpet case and took his shining golden trumpet from its bed of scarlet velvet. The beautiful new instrument gave him confidence. He worked the valves nimbly with his fingers and looked up at Mrs. Quaver again.

"Now, John," she said, "tell me when your little solo begins."

"Right after the end of the second verse," John promptly replied. He had practiced his part every evening in the basement at home for the last two weeks. He knew every note perfectly. "After the line, 'That's the way for Billy and me.' "

"Good," Mrs. Quaver said. "And don't

forget what I told you, John. This is a *happy* song. I want you to play *tah*-tuh, *tah*-tuh, *tah*-tuh-tuh, *ta-a-ah*, simply repeating the rhythm of the voice. And I want you to be light and lively. This is supposed to be the song of a boy who loves romping in the country."

Tah-tuh, *tah*-tuh, *tah*-tuh-tuh, *ta-a-ah*, John thought. That shouldn't be too difficult, even with the whole orchestra listening to him. He had played it over and over again at home. But he would have to try extra hard here. This was to be his first solo. Everyone else was depending on him to play it properly.

"Right," said Mrs. Quaver brightly. With her baton, she rapped twice sharply on the music stand before her. All the musicians brought their instruments into playing position. Susan poised her bow over the strings of her violin. John held his trumpet close to his mouth and wiggled his fingers on the valves.

Mrs. Quaver's baton moved from side to side, up, and then down! The cymbals clashed and the drums thumped. The pianist brought his fingers down on the ivory keys of the piano. The violinists and cellists made their wheeing and whumping sounds. All were in perfect unison. The rehearsal had begun.

After the introduction, one of the older boys began to sing.

"Where the pools are bright and deep,
  Where the gray trout lies asleep,
  Up the river and over the lea,
  That's the way for Billy and me."

After the last line of the first verse, John's fellow trumpeter echoed the rhythm of the singer's voice. *Tah*-tuh, *tah*-tuh, *tah*-tuh-tuh, *tah-a-ah!*

Mrs. Quaver smiled approvingly at the successful performance and, with her baton, gave the singer the signal to begin the second verse.

"Where the blackbird sings the latest,"

(An oboe went *pe-e-e-p.*)

"Where the hawthorn blooms
    the sweetest,
  Where the nestlings chirp and flee,"

(The flute warbled according to plan.)

"That's the way for Billy and me-e-e-e!"

John swallowed with an effort and put the mouthpiece of his trumpet to his lips for his solo. The mouthpiece instantly changed to chocolate. Then, almost as fast, the chocolate spread along the instrument, changing all the flashing gold into dull brown.

The first note came out fairly true. *Tah*— But chocolate trumpets cannot withstand much pressure. The hole in the mouthpiece softened and clogged up, and the valves stuck as John desperately tried to finish his part.

Mrs. Quaver's eyes almost popped out of her head as she listened to him play.

Tah-
     tuh,
        too-
           tuh,
              ter-t-t-
                t-t-
                   t-

It sounded as though John were trying to play a soap-filled bubble pipe. Terribly flustered, he put down his trumpet.

Mrs. Quaver was speechless. The orchestra was rocked by uproarious laughter. The other trumpeter leaned over toward John's chair and picked up the trumpet. "It's a chocolate trumpet!" he shouted derisively. "No wonder it sounded like that! John Midas was trying to play a chocolate—"

John didn't wait to hear any more. He fled from the stage and out to the playground. Without stopping even to look around, he ran through the stone gateway and homeward.

9

Oh, the shame of it! The humiliation! John wept breathlessly as he ran, shocked and frightened, indignant and angry at the world that had suddenly turned against him.

Mean old things, John thought, blaming Miss Plimsole and Mrs. Quaver for his failures, even though nothing that had happened to him had been their fault in any way.

Horrible old school, he thought, even though he had liked school until that morning. Hateful Susan, he thought, even though he knew at the same time that he was really longing for her to be friendly with him again.

Through the window Mrs. Midas saw John coming up the pathway. "Hello, John dear," she called from the living room. "You're home early today. How nice! As a reward, there'll be a piece of chocolate after supper."

"I hate it!" John shouted. He was crying too hard to say anything else for a moment.

When she heard the sound of his voice, Mrs. Midas rushed into the hall. "Why, what's the matter, dear?" she asked, putting her arm around him. John twisted away from her grasp, ran past her, and started up the stairs toward his bedroom.

"Susan doesn't want me at her birthday party," he said as he went. "I know she doesn't. Well, I don't want to go to her rotten old party, anyway!"

"I don't think you really mean that," Mrs. Midas said. "Besides," she added, and John was halted by the softness of her voice, "Mrs.

Buttercup just telephoned to say she was going to drive over herself at four o'clock to pick you up."

"She did?" John said, blinking down at his mother from the top of the stairway.

"Yes, she did," Mrs. Midas assured him. "So you'd better hurry and get yourself washed and brushed. Your party clothes are laid out on your bed."

There were games on the Buttercups' lawn while it was still warm enough outside. Later the party supper, including the birthday cake, was going to be served indoors, and there would be a magician and a short movie.

John joined in the blindman's buff, and grandmother's footsteps, and fox and geese, and soon he became more cheerful. He even temporarily forgot about chocolate.

Susan looked very pretty. Her yellow curls had been brushed so hard that they looked silkier than ever. She was wearing a big blue ribbon the same color as her eyes. Her cheeks were flushed with excitement—a deeper pink than her new party dress. On her feet were dainty little white socks and white shoes with straps that buttoned.

Between games, Susan smiled at John and said, "I'm glad you came." They seemed to be on good terms again.

Then Mr. Buttercup approached, bringing a bucket of water from the garage. He set it down in the middle of the lawn without spilling a single drop.

"We're going to duck for apples," Susan whispered to John, "the boys against the girls. You can be captain of the boys' team."

The two teams lined up for the race, Susan leading the girls and John the boys.

"The idea is this," Mr. Buttercup explained. "When I say go—not yet, John!— Susan and John will run to the bucket. There are twelve apples floating in the bucket and twelve people in the race. Using only their teeth, Susan and John will grab their apples and run back to their lines. As soon as they touch the hands of the Number Two runners in their teams—Dinny and Duncan—Susan and John will go to the end of their lines, and Dinny and Duncan will run to the bucket to duck for apples. Do you all understand the way it's going to work? All right! One to get ready, two to get steady, and three to—go!"

Susan bounded ahead like a jackrabbit and

had her face deep in the bucket by the time John reached her side and crouched down for his apple. He got his eye on a big red one with its stalk jutting up conveniently for him to grab. He lowered his face, opened his mouth, and lunged. Somehow his nose reached the apple before his teeth did and pushed it below the surface of the water. John's mouth followed the apple down.

Then a terrible thing happened. The clear water in the bucket turned into dark-brown, sweet, liquid chocolate. Susan and John immediately pulled their heads up. But it was too late. Their faces were drenched with chocolate syrup.

"Oh!" Susan exclaimed, wiping chocolate out of her eyes. Chocolate syrup dripped down all over her delicate pale-pink dress. "Oh!" she moaned.

John was in the same state. There was chocolate all over his face; there was chocolate on his white shirtfront and on his gray flannel shorts. And there was chocolate in his mouth. "Glug," John said. "Glug!"

Susan was too surprised and angry to speak. For the second time that day she

turned her back on John and ran away from him.

Mrs. Buttercup offered to clean John up. But he couldn't bear to stay at the party another minute. He started off at once for home.

10

Dragging along and thinking of all the dreadful things that had happened, John had walked about halfway home when he heard the cheery voice of his father.

"Hello, hello!" called Mr. Midas, crossing over from the other side of the street. He was on his way home from the station. "You left the party rather early, didn't you? What—!" Mr. Midas had just seen the patches and streaks of chocolate that were drying on John's face and on his clothes. "Good gracious!" he said. "No wonder you left the party early. How did *that* happen?"

John burst into tears. It had all been so awful. But now he could tell his father about his terrible day. He stopped crying and only sniffed a little now and then as he told the whole story—about taking the coin to the candy store, about buying the box that had turned out to have only one chocolate in it, about the toothpaste, about breakfast, the gloves, the silver dollar, the pencil, the lunch, the trumpet, and finally the apple-ducking water.

"You mean to tell me they really all turned to chocolate?" Mr. Midas asked. "You're sure you didn't imagine some of this?"

"Oh, no," John assured him.

"Well," Mr. Midas said, still looking doubtful, "we're only a couple of blocks from that candy store of yours—not that I've ever noticed one there. Suppose we stroll over and ask the man whether his chocolates always do strange things to people?"

"It's on the next corner," John said, recognizing some of the houses on the side street. "Not the next house, not the next house, not the next," he said, "but . . ." John's voice faded into silence.

The corner where he had found the candy store was nothing now but an empty lot—flat, open ground littered with a pile of rusty tin cans and broken bottles around a splintery old sign saying *For Sale.*

"Hmm," said Mr. Midas, frowning anxiously at John. "I think we'd better pay a visit to Dr. Cranium before we go home."

"That's where the store was, though," John protested, beginning to cry again. He had shed more tears in that one day, it seemed, and certainly eaten more chocolate, than in all the other days of his life put together. "I know it was."

Dr. Cranium was a busy man. As luck would have it, however, he was able to see Mr. Midas and John almost at once.

"Well, well, well, well, well!" said Dr.

Cranium. "And how are we getting along now, John? Have we cut down on our candy, eh?"

"How do you do?" John responded dully.

"Apparently he's had a bad day, Dr. Cranium," Mr. Midas said. "Trouble at school, you know. And a little accident at a birthday party. What I'm worried about is that he keeps saying that everything he puts into his mouth turns to chocolate."

"No more than a nursery fantasy, I'm sure," Dr. Cranium said to Mr. Midas. "Well, John," he went on, looking down with a smile, "suppose you tell me in your own words what the matter seems to be."

"Everything I put into my mouth turns to chocolate," John explained. "Everything I eat and everything I drink changes into chocolate. I'm thirsty. And I'm getting a pain. A bad one, I think."

Dr. Cranium sighed patiently and invited John to open his mouth and say *ah*.

"Ah," John said.

Dr. Cranium peered into John's mouth briefly and gave a low whistle of surprise. "This chocolate eating simply must stop." He went to a supply cabinet. "I don't think there's any time to be lost," he told Mr. Midas. "I'm going to give the boy some of my own special compound—Dr. Cranium's Elixir, I call it. Never fails."

Dr. Cranium selected a large bottle from one of the cabinet's crowded shelves. He removed the top from the bottle. He got a spoon from another shelf. He filled the spoon with an oily greenish-yellowish medicine that had yellowish-reddish lights glinting in it. "It doesn't taste very pleasant," Dr. Cranium warned John in a pleasant tone of voice. "But I'm sure it'll do the trick. Clear the stomach and you clear the mind. That's what I always say."

Dr. Cranium offered John the brimful spoon.

"Must I?" John asked his father. "I know it'll turn into chocolate."

"Go on." Mr. Midas nodded encouragingly. "Drink it down."

John took the spoon between his lips. The medicine turned to chocolate. The spoon turned to chocolate. John choked and spluttered, and chocolate syrup spurted from his mouth.

Dr. Cranium dropped the spoon in alarm.

When it struck the white-tiled floor, the chocolate handle snapped into several pieces. "Mercy!" said Dr. Cranium. "I've never seen anything like it! The boy's whole system seems to be so chocolatified that it chocolatifies everything it touches."

After he had recovered somewhat, the doctor went on. "I believe that this must be an unprecedented case of . . . er . . . chocolatitis. I shall call it Cranium's Disease. I shall want to make an exhaustive study of the child. I—"

"I think John has had enough excitement for one day," Mr. Midas said.

11

Mrs. Midas was much upset when Mr. Midas told her that John had Dr. Cranium's Disease.

"He said it was chocolatitis," Mr. Midas explained, a worried frown on his face. "But he's calling it Cranium's Disease, because it was his discovery."

"Dr. Cranium didn't do it," John said. "It's magic. It all started after I ate that chocolate .... I'm scared," he added.

Mrs. Midas sat down and dabbed her eyes with a lace handkerchief. She was crying.

Mr. Midas blew his nose, said he had to attend to something, and abruptly left the room.

John had been so busy feeling sorry for himself that he had not realized how his mother and father would feel about his chocolate disease. "Never mind, Mother," he said, putting his arm around her shoulders. "It's all right." Really, nothing was all right, but he couldn't bear to see his mother's tears.

He kissed her wet cheek. His eyes were shut as his lips softly touched her, so he didn't see the change right away. Then his lips began to feel sticky. He opened his eyes. His mother had turned into a lifeless statue of chocolate!

John ran wildly out of the house without thinking where he was going or what he was going to do. All he knew was that somehow he must get help. For the first time in a long while he forgot about himself altogether. Now he didn't care about anything but bringing his mother back to life. Without quite knowing how he got there, John found himself at the corner where he had bought the chocolate box. The lot was no longer an untidy rubbish dump. The neat red-brick building with two show windows was exactly where it had been in the first place. But the display of candy he had previously seen in the windows was no longer there. In one window John saw a chocolate trumpet, a chocolate pencil, and a silver dollar with a piece bitten out of it. In the other window he saw a cafeteria tray littered with chocolate utensils and the remains of a chocolate lunch. Clearly, this place was the right one. Clearly, the proprietor must know a lot about John's hateful chocolate touch. John rushed into the store.

The proprietor was standing behind the counter, carefully polishing something small and round and flat and silver. "I was just thinking of you," he said.

John had no time to waste on pleasantries. "Remember-the-old-coin-I-found-and-gave-you-and-you-gave-me-a-magic-chocolate?" he demanded. Without waiting for a reply, he babbled on. "I-ate-it-and-it-made-every-thing-that-touches-my-mouth-turn-to-chocolate-and-I-kissed-my-mother-and-now-she's-chocolate-and-I've-got-to-change-her-back!"

"Easy now," murmured the storekeeper. "Calm yourself." There was an expression of satisfaction in the old man's eyes.

"It's all your fault," John declared. "If my mother isn't made better again, I'll fight you till you're dead!"

"My goodness!" the storekeeper exclaimed. "Whose fault, did you say?"

"Yours!" John said. "If you hadn't taken that money, I wouldn't have—"

"Now, John," the storekeeper interrupted, "I must insist on honesty. I'm glad to hear that you're thinking about your mother for a change. Unselfishness is important. But honesty is also important. If you'll be truthful, perhaps I can help you."

John's ears reddened. It was becoming unmistakably evident to him that he had only himself to blame for all this unhappiness. He looked straight into the storekeeper's eyes. "I'll do anything. I'll work for you all my life for nothing, if you'll turn my mother back. You can turn me to chocolate, instead, if you want. You—"

The storekeeper apparently ignored John's

offers. "You were right, John," he said, "when you guessed that I had something to do with your acquiring the chocolate touch. But you yourself earned the coin that bought the chocolate touch. Only greedy people can even see that kind of money. Dr. Cranium was right, up to a point. I suppose that one could say that you had chocolatitis. But it was just an outward sign of selfishness."

"My mother!" John reminded the store-keeper frantically. "My mother's turned to chocolate! Do something about it! Oh, please do something about it!"

"I'm glad that you are concerned," the storekeeper commented unhurriedly. "Part of your cure is to be concerned about other people. You have been so greedy that you didn't care what happened to other people."

"Oh, I know, I know," John admitted woe-fully. "But please decide about me later. And please make my mother better now."

"Well, John," the storekeeper said, "if you had to choose between getting rid of your chocolate touch and restoring your mother to life, which would it be?"

For one moment John couldn't help imag-ining a future of all-chocolate meals. The thought was terrible. But then he thought of his mother as she had been when he had left her, a motionless chocolate statue, unable to speak, her chocolate hand still holding her lace handkerchief. Without further hesitation, John said, "Help my mother."

"Well, John," the storekeeper said, "I am going to give you another chance. When next you go to school, your chocolate pencil will be a real wooden pencil with lead in it."

"But—" John began to protest. What did the pencil matter?

"The chocolate knife and fork and spoon you left on your tray in the cafeteria will have turned back to metal. Your chocolate trumpet will be a shiny golden one again."

"But—" John said.

"Don't worry about Dr. Cranium's spoon. He will find a whole silver one on the floor, where the broken chocolate one lay."

"But how about—?" John said.

"Susan Buttercup will discover that the chocolate stains on her party dress and her shoes were nothing but water, after all. Her silver dollar will be all right."

John could stand the suspense no longer.

"My mother!" he shouted. "What about my mother? Will *she* be all right?"

The storekeeper smiled. "Why don't you run along home and find out?" he suggested.

John turned without even saying good-bye and ran out of the store.

The storekeeper went back to the disk that he had been polishing, a disk the size of a quarter. It had to be polished smooth, ready for a new set of initials in case the need for them should arise.

12

The front door was open and John rushed into the living room, where he had left his mother. She was not there now, but on the chair was a small, wet lace handkerchief. John ran into the dining room and on to the kitchen. As he came to the kitchen door, he heard the ring of silver against crockery. Then he saw a wonderful sight—his mother arranging the coffee things on a tray!

He dashed into the kitchen and flung his arms around his mother's waist, sobbing and laughing with relief and joy.

"There, there," said Mrs. Midas, stroking the hair from John's forehead. "You've had a very disturbing day, dear. But in a few minutes we're all going to have supper and everything will be fine again. Goodness! I do believe I need some coffee myself. I felt so strange just then in the other room. I really don't know what came over me."

The door from the garden opened, and Mr. Midas came in.

"Before we settle down," Mrs. Midas said to John, "have a glass of good, cold milk. You look so hot."

So they didn't know what had happened to her! Well, John thought, he certainly wouldn't scare them by telling them. He watched gratefully as his mother took a frosty blue jug from the refrigerator and poured from it a glassful of icy, creamy milk.

Trembling with nervousness, John tilted the glass against his open mouth. The liquid

flowed in and down his throat—and remained purely milky, deliciously milky, tasting of nothing but fresh, clean milk.

After the first long, wonderful gulps, he suddenly recalled that he had not thanked the storekeeper for saving his mother. "Mother," he said, "may I go out for a minute? I'll be right back."

"All right, John," she said, "but supper will be ready in ten minutes. Don't keep us waiting."

John ran briskly down the street until he came to the corner where he always turned right when he was going to Susan's house. There he turned left instead and started along the two blocks of unfamiliar street leading to the candy store. Soon he came to the corner where the red-brick building had been.

But there was no building and no store and, of course, no storekeeper. In the corner lot there was nothing to be seen but a heap of rusty tin cans and broken bottles surrounding a signboard with new lettering that said— *Sold*.

ABOUT THE AUTHOR

Born in London, Patrick Skene Catling was educated there and at Oberlin College in the United States. As a Royal Canadian Air Force navigator and as a journalist, he has traveled extensively. His present home is in the Republic of Ireland.

The original appearance of *The Chocolate Touch* in 1952 stirred much reviewer enthusiasm. *The New York Herald Tribune* remarked, "it has already proved a hilarious success with children," and *The Saturday Review* said, "it is told with an engaging humor that boys and girls will instantly discover and approve."

ABOUT THE ILLUSTRATOR

After receiving her B.F.A. from Pratt Institute in 1969, Margot Apple attended the Penland School of Crafts in North Carolina and subsequently established herself as a freelance illustrator in the fields of publishing, advertising, and greeting card design. Recently she has illustrated *Soft House* by Steve Futterman.

An advocate of self-sufficient living, Ms. Apple grows and preserves her own food and sews her own clothes. She now lives in Pittsfield, Massachusetts.